Praise for *Now That I Am Older*

Myrne Roe is a writer. Her poems get to the very heart of things. Whether she is talking about a funeral—her own—or squirrels, or pondering a wedding ceremony and how fleeting life's defining moments are, or just what it is like to live a full and examined life, her wisdom and inner truth is a salve to me. It will be to you, too.
  —*Sarah Bagby*, *Owner, Watermark Books & Café, Wichita*

Myrne Roe uses crisp imagery to explore aging: "Gold gifts lost in places I cannot point to / I can only remember the brilliance of what has gone." Comedy: "The girl had the glazed look of a lost mall shopper." And candor: "If we live long enough we move from being a child to being a child again. Mother is all the evidence I need." You will see yourself in her writing.
  —*Kelly Johnston*, *Fellow poet; author of "Kalaska" and "Tumbleweed"*

This book is full of sweet and poignant storytelling in poems and prose. For the author, it is a synopsis of her work using written words to express her own thoughts and those of others. For the reader, it is an honest look at life and the relationships, trials, and tribulations that can affect us most. Whatever stage of life you are currently in, you will find an inspirational short story or poem here. You will not want to put it down!
  —*Melody J. Cole*, *Author of* Sentiments of a Survivor

Wit and wisdom shine in stories that reflect lives of a generation. Roe's poetry extrapolates a gem from each experience drawing one into a vivid tapestry of emotions.

—*Margalee Wright*, *Former Mayor City of Wichita*

Myrne Roe writes with such honesty, insight, humor, and lyrical brevity that each piece causes reflection, recognition, smiles, and, sometimes, laughter. In "Waning Virtue" we are the child led by an older child into truths we had been protected from. In "Family" small details tell the story of parents' power and self-deception (e.g., Grandma drowned wearing her veiled hat because she never learned to swim.)

"Recurring Dreams" names our shared dreams, no less fearful because we share them. "Family Trust" and "Birthstone" are bookends: the damage done and the help offered without words by family. "Untitled," "Vista," and "Spider Tracks" are mirrors in which we see ourselves with brutal honesty. "Marriage" and "Cityscape" among others reveal the deep satisfaction of loving. "Writing While Walking" is any writer's best advice, shown, not told.

My favorites among the short stories are "The Sewing Room," "The 1953 Wellington Wheat Festival," "Two-Headed Calf," and "Before it Gets Dark." Like her poems, Roe's stories are carefully crafted without extra words. Up close we see truths and are moved. I will reread this book again and again.

—*Gretchen Cassel Eick*, *Professor of history; author of eight books*

Experience the humor, grief, wonder, and grit Myrne Roe expresses in *Now That I Am Older*. Her pieces are accessible to all, even those people who have thought they either don't like or don't understand poetry. You will have a remarkable experience.

—**Marietta Anderson**, *Writer and communication strategist*

. . . when Myrne worked at the *Wichita Eagle* she proved to be one of the most insightful people I've ever known. She was ever mindful of the importance of the printed word. When she complimented me on a column, it made my day.

—**Bonnie Bing**, *Freelance writer and* Wichita Eagle *columnist*

NOW
THAT
I AM OLDER

ALSO BY MYRNE ROE

BOOKS

Under Hope's Roof, compiler and editor
Radiating Like a Stone: Wichita Women and the 1970s Feminist Movement, compiler and editor

POETRY CHAPBOOK

Ironing Out the Wrinkles

ANTHOLOGY INCLUSIONS

"Before It Gets Dark" in *Everyday Tales: A Small Book about Lindsborg, a Small Kansas Town*, Shannon Littlejohn, editor
"Udall, Kansas," "Winter's Truths," "1953 Wellington Wheat Festival" in *Kansas Time+Space: An Anthology of Heartland Poetry*, Roy Beckemeyer and Caryn Mirriam-Goldberg, editors

PLAYS

Reader's theater production: *"What Do You Want to Be When You Grow Up, Little Girl?"*
One woman show: *"Several of My Sisters"*

NOW

THAT

I AM OLDER

POEMS AND SHORT STORIES

MYRNE ROE

With a Foreword by Roy J. Beckemeyer

Author photo by Patty Ringgenberg
Cover design by BespokeBookCovers.com
Public domain line drawings courtesy of vecteezy.com

ISBN: 979-8-9875793-2-9

Post Rock Press
PO Box 24314, Knoxville, TN 37933
Postrockpress.org

This book is dedicated to my late husband of 59 years Jon Roe, an award-winning journalist, our much-loved son Matthew, and my sister Jane Hicks.

FOREWORD

An Appreciation of *Now That I Am Older* by Myrne Roe

In the very first poem, "Gems," in Myrne Roe's new book *Now That I Am Older,* she opens by using the highly detailed specificity of a list of jewelry she has lost, expressed in what seems an oft-recollected sequence of mental images in a stream-of-consciousness-syntax ("...Gift from my love somewhere / between a Chicago bar and performance / by Julie Harris who had a stroke / and didn't appear / an understudy did..."), to remind us how we wander through our lives remembering moments with such exquisite clarity that we cannot understand how the rock-like solidity of lost treasures could have slipped away beneath our notice. The last three lines of this semi-precious stone of a poem encapsulate perfectly what she has been leading us to with each subsequent example: "I can only remember / the brilliance of what has gone knowing / too late it's the real thing." Those of you who, like this reviewer, have also accumulated a certain abundance of years will appreciate that this level of astuteness is as often followed abruptly by a blinding reminder of how so many of our touchstones are now fading into the mists and myths of history. The second poem, "Buying My Buddy Holly Glasses," begins "Who, said the sales girl, is Buddy Holly?"

And we know that girl, who "had the glazed look / of a lost mall shopper," likely won't even bother to google "Buddy Holly."

Myrne Roe's years of writing masterful prose and explication and lyricism, provide both the elbow grease and the innate artistic ability to buff each poem and story in this delightful little book to near perfection. Here we find humor ("…good friends / who seem more like family than the family I / never hear from except in a Christmas form letter"), empathy ("No living being / should live in abandonment with / no one to answer, no one to care"), and wisdom ("Life does not hang in a museum / It does not decorate a wall or wait on an easel").

And at the end, in the final poem in what may be her final book, Myrne completes the cycle, coming back to her opening theme: "Your earrings are the real deal, / my sister told me on Christmas Day, / Don't lose one… / …I vow / these gems will not be lost. / They signal the end to winter's storms, / welcome the lilac's bloom."

In *Now That I Am Older*, Myrne Roe proffers us the captivating glimmer of moments, insights, smiles, tears; a treasure chest of words and imagery to enjoy over and over again, each time we open its cover.

Roy J. Beckemeyer
Author of *The Currency of His Light* (Turning Plow Press, 2023)

CONTENTS

Comings and Goings

GEMS

I lose jewelry.
Diamond tennis bracelet
Gift from my love somewhere
between a Chicago bar and performance
by Julie Harris who had a stroke
and didn't appear
an understudy did. Ruby
pendant while dining
at the London Ritz or listening
to a Bobby Short would-be
at the Savoy whichever one
it did not return to me.
Grandmother's amber stone
and seed pearl pin lost in charity
sweaters perfect on a beige one
I never cared for
and could not retrieve. Gold
gifts lost in places
I cannot point to and say
who after me has my ring,
broach or earring.
I can only remember
the brilliance of what has gone knowing
too late it's the real thing.

BUYING MY BUDDY HOLLY GLASSES

Who, said the salesgirl, is Buddy Holly?
Died in a plane crash,
Clear Lake, Iowa.
The Big Bopper died too
And another singer I cannot recall.

The girl had the glazed look
of a lost mall shopper.
Pale beige hair stood up
like toothpicks stuck in her skull,
a gold globe earring pierced her nose.

After heating and torturing
my new glasses to fit my face,
she scrutinized my trifocal, bifocal lines.

I stared back at her through
my new black big-rims.

It's So Easy was a great success
One of his best, I said.
His band was called the Crickets.

4

In her eyes I saw
Boredom? Wariness?

She looked away.
Have a nice day.

      Peggy Sue was a good song, too.
      You'd probably like it.

I left humming *That'll Be the Day.*

Ergo Ego

I am a balloon
inflated,
floating
until cooling air
or clumsily tied string
steals my loft,
sends me to the floor
to lie flat
unless someone
pumps me up,
carefully seals
my essence
and even then
I will not
last forever.

FOLK ART

is a practical art by people
who decline instruction
and notions of greatness.

They scoop up earth, mix in rain,
sculpt a jar for cooling milk.
Create water fowl from driftwood.
Carve small treasures with folding knives.

Invent color with growing things.
Paint it on debris.
Leave behind the only semblance
of Father and the family dog.

SUMMER MUSE '39

Grandmother plied a visitor with sweet potatoes, homegrown
green beans cooked with bacon fat, meatloaf with gravy.
A hearty meal for the man
who stood at her back door with pleading eyes.
Milk from a bottle, a slice of rhubarb pie
just as we had eaten at her table
before our cleaning up and Sunday rest.
He left no morsel. Our scraps went into a rusted can
he took to feed the chickens. He chopped wood
enough to fill the space beneath back porch steps.
We children shed to our skivvies to sleep on a pallet
while the adults sat under the front yard oak sipping tea.
Grandmother watched the man smoke a hand rolled cigarette.
He told her he'd slept two nights under a railroad trestle
next to a creek, caught a catfish, had it for supper.
He was on his way west he said to find work,
maybe start farming again. She thought times
were the worst she'd known but she had a roof over her head.
The grandchildren had shoes for school.
Would he like another piece of pie, a sandwich to take with him?

Thanks, he said. Good food. Been a pleasure.

She sat on the steps and stared at the place he had sat.

The shifting wind ruffled her hair. The sun surprised her cheek.

Grandmother ran to the road, past the adults who stared,

and called to the man walking toward the tracks.

What's your name? He did not answer.

When the train whistled he, too, began to run.

PLAYER

In the first act
I traversed the aisle
To mmmm and ooooo sounds
adults make when observing
clever children.
Sang God eyeballs sparrow.
My mother who arranged my first gig
told me that everyone (bird and girl child)
is watched over by Him.
Be on your best behavior
or He will swat your behind.

Curtain rises on deep waters.
My soul agonizes,
flails and flounders toward shore.
I keep my head up, learn
acting and stay afloat.

A sparrow feeds at the tray
I readied with seeds.
Another bathes in the shell-shaped bath
the night rain prepared.
Deus ex machina.
I've found the meaning of my song.

SEASONS

The squirrel pauses, her face framed
against her tail, amber in the late sun.
Winter will not take her by surprise.
Paws in prayerful triangle, my neighbor
has faith she can balance on high wires,
race to a single thin branch, leap
to another.
A brain twitch sends her off
to bury treasure in sight of her nest
where babies will birth.
If the burly dog shakes off rest, ambles
out of his yard into mine, she will zip
up a tree—pose nose down—
berate the yawning beast.
When I turn off my light
just before the moon rises, she sleeps.
That's where I want to go,
where time sprints as a squirrel.

OBITUARY

Who knows when an attack
or simply lightning
will send you, my family, scrambling.
Please don't write about my jobs
or the honors in basement boxes.
List only the relatives I like and a couple of good friends
who seem more like family than the family I
never hear from except in a Christmas form letter.
Refrain from telling my story
that way—relating lore of clever offspring
and expensive vacations. Mention, instead,
how the dog enjoys trips to the bank drive-through.
Omit how I am a loving mother and faithful wife,
although I am. That's to be expected.
Nothing of hobbies which have been varied whims.

Rather, make my newspaper farewell speak to what
I became after sixty years and a good anti-depressant.
How I learned to write poetry and embrace
afternoon naps after reading
fiction without socially redeeming value.

Speak of my obsession for Scrabble, loose clothes in soft fabric,
fresh fruit and frozen yogurt. Appreciation for bird songs,
road trips, movies starring Tom Hanks, CDs by Diana Krall
and my great nephew's baby grip on my finger while I imitate
duck sounds that make him laugh. Explain how
my husband's kisses and my son's puns make me happy,
how art gives me pause.

As to the funeral, make it modest. Gather where my
ashes are scattered, listen to bagpipes of Amazing Grace
and toast my discovery of what is life's best time.
Pour a glass of white wine and allow
it to trickle over my remains. Finally,
tell some jokes. Someone should mention
how funny I can be, quote my finest one-liners.
The best sendoff would be laughter.

LOST

First it was two dots of sound,
harsh, frenetic, afraid.
As the goose came closer,
the two dots got louder, a solo
goose, gander, or gosling
flying erratically, side to side
low, higher, never a straight line.
Each time it cried, the sounds
became more heartbreaking.
It was not a recluse by choice.
How was it left behind?
Was he too busy with his head beneath
a wing preening? Was he sleeping
unaware the flock had moved on?
Was he too far on the lake swimming,
bathing, diving for food? Too young
to know better than lag behind.
I watched him disappear into the heavens,
an aimless flight.

If I had wings, I would have followed the goose,
offering comfort, joining in the hunt
for company. Teach goose calls
of conversation. Ensure familiarity,
family and home. No living being
should live in abandonment with
no one to answer, no one to care.

MARRIAGE

On a feverish Kansas afternoon,
you said *with this wing I thee red.*
Reverend did not smile.
The pregnant bridesmaid swayed to hymns,
the names of which I did not know.

After too sweet cake, we ran
through raining rice and drank
warm champagne under a full moon.
Worried we could not transcend
the summer ceremony.

Why didn't we admit
the absurd in a ritual where people sweat
in their best clothes just to watch
something that isn't their business?
Run off to Reno as we discussed?

The unsmiling minister who gave me
to you is dead now. Where is the bridesmaid
who named her child Sunny? What fears
have we not survived? Is the cake
still in the freezer?

SOMEBODIES

WANING VIRTUE

My cousin came for a visit
when he was six and I was four.
He brought his cap pistol,
made me a stick weapon.

We hunted brown bears behind the garage,
greedy wolves that circled the chicken coop.
We climbed the mound above the cellar door.
Rolled down, climbed up again.

He made hissing sounds, said snakes were near.
I giggled till my sides were sore.
We followed a forbidden path to the creek
and watched water beings flit and whirl.

Tadpoles grow to be frog moms and dads, he declared.
He whispered truths about Santa and elves,
Easter bunnies who laid pastel eggs,
a fairy who bought young teeth for a dime.

My world spun faster, flung me past
my parents who sought to shield me
from wild beasts, forbidden cellar doors,
creeks fed by new storms.

GRANDMA BONE MOVES TO FLORIDA

What's he saying Grandma Bone asks
looking through smudged glasses,
hearing aid squealing. *My chair* she murmurs
as the auctioneer sells
her life for less than what it means.
She pulls her sweater tight across her chest.
You won't need that in Florida
her daughter teases. The old woman
turns away, sees a girl with bric-a-brac.
Sees a man with her husband's satchel.
Going, going, gone.

THE TWO-HEADED CALF

"Pampaw, me go too."

Before he could pick up the child, his wife's voice cut through the morning air, "Don't let her outside, Horace. She don't need to see it."

"She won't notice."

"She'll notice enough."

"Stay inside, Pumpkin Pie. Grandma wants you to keep her company. Besides it looks like it's going to rain."

The child's lower lip poked out. "See Dr. Dog Cat."

"It's Dr. Doggett and you can see him later after he's done helping Maude." Pumpkin sat down hard on the linoleum and started to kick her legs, but Horace pretended not to notice, carefully closing the screen door to avert her escalating temper.

"Warm out here for March." Doggett was sweating as he worked over the exhausted cow and her two-headed calf. "What do ya wanna do, Horace? Kill it? Keep it? I've been feeding it some out of a bottle, but it don't seem to get the hang of it. Even if it learns to eat, it won't live until it's full grown. Don't think it's hurting any."

Horace leaned on the stall and scratched behind his ear. A self-absorbed barn cat was cleaning herself not five feet from the deformed calf. "You know, Doc, it's actually kinda cute."

"Well, it's not worth much, that's for sure except maybe for that Pritchard fellow out near the state line would buy it for his highway freak show. He's already got a five-legged sheep and some rattlesnakes. I hear tell he lost his cow with three eyes. Could probably use another cow and, to my way of thinking, two heads is a better draw than three eyes."

Horace wiped his face with his bandana. He didn't like the feel of things. It was too sticky warm for an early hour. Even warmer than in the summer when, like now, the sun was still a mass of reds and pinks hovering on the horizon. And now the gray was moving closer.

"Now come look at this." Doggett gestured toward the calf's torso." It's pretty well-formed except for this extra head thing. Kinda spooky though. Not natural."

A startling boom of thunder caused Maude to stir on her straw bed and the calf to lift one head ever so slightly.

"Hell," Doggett said, "the thing can hear."

Horace moved to the doorway. To the west, behind the house, he saw a bank of churning green-black clouds heading his way. Cool air flowed between layers of hot so it was possible to feel both chilled and too warm all at once. "Storm," said Horace. "Come on."

"So, what do ya wanna do? Let it starve? Shoot it?"

Lightening zigzagged and lit up his neighbor's wheat field like a ballpark. "Man, it's gonna storm bad. We'll figure out the calf later."

The rain was coming down in large drops and pea-sized hail was melting as it hit the ground. The air was heavy, pushing down on the two men as they ran toward the house. "Lena, get Pumpkin. Head for the cellar."

His wife wasn't completely dressed yet, her hair was in pin curls and she wore her house slippers. Her hands gripped the back of the child's highchair, her voice quivered. "I can't find Pumpkin. Oh dear Lord, help me. Horace, I can't find her."

Horace's eyes widened; his body tensed. "Pumpkin?" he bellowed as he started for the stairs.

"Not there. Not down here. Oh Lord, I came right down after you went outside. Wasn't but a minute or so. Oh, Lord."

The storm began beating the roof with hail, then patting it with rain. Sporadic wind gusts blew tree limbs, a trash can, and other debris against buildings, clanking and banging. It was dark and light, cold and hot, silent, and noisy.

The three grownups raced around the yard, dodging flying objects, begging the child to find them. The grandmother's keening clashed with the men's low and loud cries. The storm and the terrified three made sorrowful music.

Abruptly the storm paused, allowing a grace period when each one heard Pumpkin call from the barn. "Me, Maude and baby, and Kitty here, Pampaw."

Doggett found her first. He scooped her up. Horace grabbed the cat and his wife's hand. They were in the storm cellar only seconds before the backside of the plummeting, swirling winds sucked up the house, the barn, and Doggett's new van.

When the four of them came out of the cellar to examine the storm's consequences, they were amazed to find Maude standing where they had left her, one head of the calf getting its breakfast.

Horace picked up his granddaughter and brushed her bangs away from her wide eyes. "You know, Pumpkin, I believe we got us a two-headed calf."

Doggett walked over to where his van had been. He sighed and shook his head. Not a tire track, nothing.

Lena fell to her knees, giving in to great sobs of fear and relief. Horace reached down to help her up. "We're not dust yet," he said. "It's a mess, but by God, Lena, look at your garden. Not a rose or lilac bush down, not a plant touched. Hell, I bet you can still get a good crop of rhubarb growing there."

"Look at your garden, Grandma. Look at yum-yum rhubarb," the little girl implored.

Horace laughed. "She hates rhubarb," he told Doggett, preoccupied with looking for his steering wheel, a hubcap, anything.

"I guess I'd better start walking down the road. Probably some animals hurt in all this," he told Harold. "I'll be needed. I'll send someone to help around here."

The sun continued its progression overhead. The barn cat sauntered over and rubbed against Horace's leg. A chicken, feathers ruffled, pecked at the ground near the garden.

THE LIFE OF BILL

Bill sat on the front porch swing staring
at the faded red paint under his feet.
Whole house needs painting he thought,
didn't feel any immediate action was necessary.
Only painted once in all the years they had lived there
when his wife nagged him to do it.
He chuckled to himself. Her nagging
was about the only communication they had.
His ancient Ford pickup sat in the driveway.
Last he drove it, was to the hospital and
road to the cemetery with the preacher.
Ford's been sitting there for so long; the battery is dead.
The sun was barely above the horizon
making everything pink and blue, two blues actually,
one baby boy blue, the other navy.
His lunch pail was by his side.
He'd made the same lunch since his wife died.
Coffee in the thermos with two spoons of sugar,
a bologna sandwich on white bread, some mustard.
Oreo cookies in a baggie. An apple today.
Probably a banana tomorrow. He liked his own cooking.

She fixed meatloaf and roast beef sandwiches
and her homemade oatmeal cookies. No matter
how many times he asked, she sent canned fruit
and he wanted fresh besides it seemed
a lot of trouble to open a can, plus the juice spilled.
The neighbor's black cat hopped up the stairs,
rubbed her back on his denim covered leg.
Dang, another rip in the hem he noticed.
He asked the cat, where is old Charlie?
His friend was always on time to drive them to work
at the lumber mill ten miles away.
Bill liked the smell of wood chips, especially maple.
Liked the fellows who worked there, too.
He heard the phone ring and pulled his foot
gently from the circle of fur.
No one ever called except someone wanting him
to go to church and Charlie who should be on the road by now.
He picked up the receiver, stopped the annoying noise in mid-
        ringing.

Bill, a woman said before he could answer.

Bill, this is Emma. Charlie's neighbor. So sorry to tell you.

A heart attack we think. Can't take you to work any more.

Bill went back to the porch, opened his lunch box, fed some
       bologna

to the cat now on the swing beside him. Ate the apple.

Might as well. He wasn't going anywhere today.

The sun was fully in the one-blue sky.

No clouds, he thought. Poured himself some coffee.

FAMILY

She punished her cuticles bloody,
required gloves. When her father threatened
the booby hatch (his words) she pulled out
her pubic hair with tweezers and
recalled her grandma wore a veiled hat
when she drowned in the cold farm pond.
Unavoidable (her mother's word)
since grandmother never learned to swim.

BEFORE IT GETS DARK

I believe it is true that if we live long enough, we move from being a child to being a child again. Mother is all the evidence I need. She looks at me through fog-covered eyes, like a baby just beginning to make out shapes and colors.

"You cut your hair?" She is showing off now, pretending she can still notice small things. At best she sees wavy, gray shadows.

"No," I say. "I just curled it today." (I had not; my hair looks as it has for nearly five years now.)

It is as if I were explaining how to use a spoon or pick up a ball. I try not to sound like that. She resents it I know, when I speak to her as she once spoke to me more than sixty years ago.

I want to make amends. "I have on new black slacks, though. They are pleated in front like your white ones."

"Aunt Margaret was too much of a lady." Mother speaks to a spot on the wall as if it was a teleprompter from which she is reading. "Once when I visited her in South Haven, I put on my cousin Billy's jeans. I stole the mule to ride into town. Well, I didn't steal it, but I didn't ask first.

"Auntie was always trying to make me a lady. I was a tomboy. I played as hard as Billy and my other cousin, Ellis. I think I was twelve. We were always playing cowboys or wrestling or swimming in the pond. I did what they did. Made her mad. Said I couldn't come visit again until I started acting like a girl."

Mother sits in her frayed brown-and-green-plaid recliner that she seldom reclines. I wait for her to continue, knowing nothing I say or do will divert her from her story until she is done with it.

"Anyway, I rode that mule downtown where there was a big fountain with water spurting out of some fish's mouth. The mule bucked me off and there I sat in Billy's pants, up to my neck in water. That mule was running around in circles." Mother laughs. No, giggles is more accurate.

"Auntie came tearing up to that fountain. She had a switch. She was madder than a hornet's nest. She wasn't mad about the mule or the fountain. She was mad that a girl—her blood kin—had on boys' pants."

Mother is tired now. It is the second time during this visit she has told me about the pants and mule and her boldness as a young girl. It is time for her to nap, but she fights off fatigue, attempting to ward off, I think, my departure.

We had gone to lunch at the Johnson City Dairy Queen. She always chooses there or, sometimes, McDonalds. She never seems to have enough hamburgers and Dr Peppers. We had filled a prescription at Wal-Mart and gone to the bank. All during lunch she talked about buying a commemorative silver dollar for John's birthday. "Get the one in the blue box," she ordered.

She was angry because I insisted on lunch before the bank errand. (Her middle-of-the-day medication has to be taken with food. And it was nearly 1 o'clock.) She sulked when we next went to Wal-Mart. (It is next door to the Dairy Queen, and the bank is across town. With the weather turning colder and with flurries in the forecast, expediting our errands seemed to me a wise decision.) She told the pharmacist her plans for the gift and the blue box it would come in. After the bank errands, she relaxed some, although she mentioned several times she didn't want the black or maroon box.

Even after we had returned to her apartment, she made me swear I had gotten the blue one.

"I have to leave in a while, Mom," I say, starting our departure ritual.

"Why?" She knows why, but she always asks anyway. My answer is always the same, and her reluctance to accept it the same as well.

"Because I need to get home before it gets dark. It takes at least two hours and it is already nearly 4 o'clock."

Mother sometimes hears what I say. It depends on whether her hearing aid is turned up, whether she is paying attention and whether she feels like hearing. She never feels like hearing that I will soon be closing her front door behind me and driving back home to Lindsborg.

"I think I liked Lindsborg best of anywhere we ever lived," she announces. "Of course, I always liked Mt. Vernon, Indiana, because our landlady was so nice and it was pretty there. Humid but pretty. Your dad hated it, though."

I glance at my watch. I can give her a few minutes of Dad-talk before I go. "Why did he hate it?"

"You know why," she snaps. And of course, I do. He hated his job in the flour mill there. He was a foreman and he didn't like bossing other men around, because he surmised they didn't like him. Dad was a man uneasy about himself.

"We always ended up back in Johnson City, no matter what. He liked this mill job best.

"He liked working in the lab, by himself," she says. She is, as always, matter-of-fact about him. She accepts that he didn't quite fit in anywhere except with her and with his garden. He grew pumpkins, radishes, onions, potatoes, tomatoes, cucumbers, and squash. "His specialties," she always says.

"His friends," I think.

We sit quietly. I worry about day-time visiting passing into night-time driving. She talks about how pretty she was when Dad was courting her. She told me about being a good dancer in high school. How all the boys wanted to dance with her. How Daddy couldn't dance worth a hoot, but she still liked him best. "He was sure a good kisser, though."

"Now Mother," I say, playing the game of a scandalized grown-up.

"He was also good. . ."

"That's enough," I say.

She acts the innocent, changes the subject. "I liked Lindsborg because it was pretty and had good schools, and people were nice to us. You and I would walk to the drugstore and have a lime Coke. Ronald Swanson was the druggist, and we sat on tall stools at the counter. You always made your stool go around too fast. Time and again I told you to stop. I swear you did it to aggravate me."

I know it will be several more minutes before I can leave with less guilt, so I reminisce with her, as she had planned I would.

"You made us matching dresses out of flour sacks."

She smiles at the memory. "I made sun dresses mostly. Your dad thought we looked cute in them. For that matter, so did I."

I, too, liked the dresses. No other Lindsborg girls and their mothers sipped lime Cokes while wearing outfits made of muslin-like cloth patterned with violets, houses, or little bears.

"And," she brags, "I made lovely quilts. Do you still have that one?"

"Which one?" I ask. "I have the one you made for your grandson with farm animals on it. And the all-blue one that's on the bed in our guest bedroom. I have at least two patch quilts and the one on our bed that's greens and browns."

"If you have too many, then give them back," she retorts.

I pick a new topic. "Remember when we lived in Lindsborg and a calf got loose down by the tracks and chased me? I was wearing roller skates attached to my saddle shoes and the skates came loose and whipped my ankles as I ran. I had bruises and cuts. I was bleeding. My skate key, on a string around my neck, flew up and loosened a baby tooth. I was always afraid of cows."

"That was the tooth you lost when you bit into a marshmallow." She stops speaking, her eyes shut and her arms hugging her chest. Over the past few months, the long breaks in conversation are more and more common. I wait. She will return to the present soon enough.

"Your dad saw the Lindsborg mayor walk by the grocery store one day. Said, 'There goes a great man.' I don't know the mayor's name. He was Swedish, of course. Everyone in Lindsborg is. Your dad was too shy to speak to him." She retreats again.

I am beginning to wear down, as I inevitably do toward the end of our visits. I get weary of her topic. I want to focus on me. On cows. On my mother's refusal to see how important my grade-school obsession was and how it colored my life at the time. After I limped for days after the calf-skate-race incident. I also suffered a bad cut (which required stitches) on my hand when I climbed up on a neighbor's shed to escape. I was rescued by two men sent to capture the animal.

Mother took me to the doctor and told him that the calf was smaller than I was, "no bigger than a kitten." Dr. Anderson laughed, so of course I loudly disputed her claim. He told me to be quiet and act like a lady. I was two times humiliated. Once by them and once by a calf.

Dad didn't say much except that I shouldn't be afraid of one of God's gentle creatures. I was only in the second grade, but I distinctly recall telling him that I thought it was better to be afraid of cows than to run from people. I suspect my memory is faulty and I didn't say such a thing. It would have hurt his feelings and he would have sulked into the evening, silent and sad.

I say to Mother, "Let's talk about the calf chasing me. I don't remember the mayor, but I can see that small brown cow with big old eyes just as if I had seen it this morning."

I pat her hand (not so as to hurt, but probably a little harder than necessary), a signal for her to pay attention. "I was terribly frightened by cows. It seems silly now, but then cows were in all

34

my nightmares." I want her understanding. I know it is getting late, but I want, before I leave, for her to be the mother for a while.

Mom looks down at her wedding ring, loose on her finger Her hands are veined and wrinkled, the skin almost transparent around several small purple splotches. She smooths her yellow-white hair and refuses to reply.

"Do you know that I was late to school almost every morning before we moved to Lindsborg, when we lived in Oklahoma?" I raise my voice to ensure she'll hear, to force her to empathize. "I went blocks and blocks out of my way so I wouldn't have to walk past two cows. One was in a pen a city block from our house. It never once acknowledged my comings and goings. But it terrified me.

"And another block down the road a cow—a large black and white one with pink udders—stood tied to a fence post. It, too, ignored me. But I was certain they would rush toward me, crushing me to death. I knew they were monsters and that they hated me. I was terrified, Mom. They made me light headed and sick to my stomach. I still don't like big, dumb cows." She looks at me with feigned innocence, erasing any chance I'd feel contrite over my outburst.

"I know," she says suddenly, leaning toward me. She is speaking quietly, slowly. "You were often frightened as a child. You didn't like the dark or thunderstorms. Fairy tales and certain radio shows, too."

She leans closer yet and raises her voice. "And you were scared to death of old Mr. Hastings with the long nose hair and crossed eyes."

I laugh. My mood goes as quickly as it came. "I'd forgotten him. He was scary. And he was always hanging out around the pool hall or the filling station. He talked to himself."

"Maybe he was lonely," she says gruffly Then she touches my hand ever so gently. (A lesson, I think, in how to pat for attention). "I didn't encourage you to be afraid of him or anything else, and I always loved you."

She resumes her straight-up posture. "I also loved your constantly frightened father. Afraid of his own shadow. Probably comes from his mother who always told him he was worthless." She is defiant, like a child defending a crayon mural on the living room wall.

"I wish you'd come live in Lindsborg with John and me," I say "Bethany Home is a wonderful place. You'd have your own room there, and we could go for rides and eat Swedish pancakes and drink lime Cokes. Lindsborg has a McDonalds and Dairy Queen now. The Wal-Mart is only a few miles away in Salina.

Our weekly visit always ends with her pronouncement of how she will stay in her own home until she can't care for herself and how she won't spoil John's and my retirement by being a burden. I respond that it was more of a burden to drive back and forth to Johnson City and that it is already very difficult for her to take care of daily chores. She ends the conversation with a dismissive, "We'll see."

She seems so frail. I worry as I would if I were leaving my son alone when he was only, say, six or seven. "What will you do tomorrow?" I know it would not be much—a day of getting dressed, fixing instant oatmeal, welcoming the friendship meals lady, and talking on the phone to me and to her sister-in-law.

"The home nurse will be here." She is obviously pleased for a change in routine even if it only means having her blood pressure taken, her medicines organized.

"Don't forget to ask her about that sore spot on your back, Mom."

"I won't."

"Would you like for me to leave her a note?" sometimes Mother wants my help and other times she doesn't. This time she does not.

"No. And I don't like wearing a button around my neck, come to think of it." (I had insisted she get one of those necklaces that she could activate if she had an accident and couldn't get up, couldn't get to the phone to call for help.)

She points a finger at me. "Next thing you know you'll get me one of those clap-hands lamps or one of those recliner chairs that dump you out on your butt when you can't get up fast."

She is clearly miffed with my assumptions about her abilities even though earlier in our visit I had helped her change her wet pants and I had cleaned out her refrigerator, disposing of sour milk, slimy lettuce, and outdated cottage cheese.

"Goodbye, Mom. I love, you," I say. "It is so late. I simply have to go."

"Watch out for the cows," she replies. She is partial to irony.

I smile and kiss her on the forehead; her skin smells faintly of baby powder. "I will," I promise "I will."

"Remember" she asks, "when we went to the Methodist Church in Lindsborg? It has those beautiful Jesus pictures by the Swedish painter?"

"Sandzen," I say. "The artist's name is Sandzen."

"Whoever. I loved that church."

"You can go there again, Mom. If you move back to Lindsborg. Please think about it. It was your favorite place to live."

"Oh, but I liked Mt. Vernon, too. Why don't I move there:" She is baiting me. Trying to hold on to me longer even if it means an argument.

"I've got to go, Mom." I kiss her again, her cheek this time. She waves me away. Under her breath, she scolds, "afraid of cows, for heaven's sakes."

Then she says, "And people. Bless his heart. He was afraid of people."

It is now 4:30. I hurry out the door. Leave her to fears of her own.

IVA DORSEY RICHARDS DIED

Brittle and blind, she told the doctor,
I was the best dancer. Told the nurse,
I once had a dress, butter yellow,
that moved with my hips.
When her children arrived
to sick-room sounds of drip, beep, whir,
she dreamed a foxtrot, danced
with their father before they knew her.

PIONEERING WOMEN

Abbie told Miranda. "Daddy is going to get some car parts in Salina. See, Mrs. Thompson looks after me most of the time when daddy can't, but her baby Tommy came down with the chicken pox and since I haven't had it yet, here I am."

The old woman figured since Abbie's mother ran off when her daughter was almost two that the child was now seven. The small suitcase by the door meant she wasn't here for a quick hello and goodbye. On previous occasions, Abbie just stood by the broken gate and waved to her.

Sometimes Miranda wondered about Abbie's sanity, the way she would wave like a scarecrow, all dangling arms and legs, head flopping side to side. Other times, she'd appear quite the sedate young lady. Once, dressed up in her mother's clothes, the little girl had feigned illness, her hand going from a somber wave to her forehead. She staggered about in dramatic distress, before running off.

Miranda sighed and, accepting her uninvited responsibility, gestured Abbie inside. "Might as well come on and get yourself settled." The front room was dark and musty with closed curtains and dusty-smelling overstuffed chairs. Abbie peered through the dimness at the five or six pictures on one wall. "You got a lot of pictures of Jesus when he was all bloody," Abbie observed.

40

But the old woman was unaware of the comment. She was pushing open the door to her kitchen, which was bright and clean with red-checkered tablecloth and curtains. The house was long like a railroad car. The next room was a bedroom. Its spare furnishings were a bed covered with a blue and brown quilt and a small chest above which hung a large gold-colored cross. The one window looked out over a white-blossomed pear tree and a giant lilac bush, filling the small space with flower perfumes, even with the window open only an inch or so.

Abbie asked, "Can I sleep here?" to insure there was no question about her aspiration, she put her two hands together as in prayer and leaned her cheek on them, closed her eyes and pretended sleep. "This way," she was told. In another room, not much bigger than a closet, Miranda pointed to the cot. "Yours," she said. Abbie plopped down on the cot to sulk, but changed her mind when the old woman walked away without noticing.

After a dinner of canned green beans, applesauce, and toast, the two returned to the front-porch glider where the old woman read her Bible and then a book about pioneers. "Our mothers and grandmothers helped settle this land." She pointed to pictures of healthy-looking muscular women plowing and cooking. She showed Abbie one of a woman firing a gun at an unseen predator.

Abbie playing with her toes and picking at peeling paint on the glider, started to get up and look for a radio, until she remembered the old woman couldn't hear. When a burst of flickering lights appeared on the lawn, Abbie touched Miranda's hand for attention. "I'm going to catch fireflies, which are really fairies." The old woman dismissed her with a nod and returned to her reading as the evening dimmed.

When morning came and the two had dressed for the day, Miranda led the way to the porch glider. On other Saturdays Abbie would go shopping with her father or play in the tree house he built. She'd read her books. If she was at Mrs. Thompson's she could play in the yard on the tree swing or in the barn where cats slept on hay bales when they weren't pursuing field mice. She tried to explain to Miranda that she was bored, that it was a nice day and that they should go for a walk. The old woman held the pioneer book closer to her face and turned her head away from the child.

So, Abbie took long steps back and forth in front of the glider, putting her hand over her eyes like an Indian guide peering in the distance until Miranda laid the book aside. "All right," she said finally, "but we can't go far. I'm old and if I fall I could break a hip." Abbie made certain she didn't speak funny when she replied, "I won't let that happen. I'll take care of you." Miranda pursed her lips and shook her head. "I doubt it," she said.

As they walked down the path under trees budding with spring, the old woman breathed in the fresh air. She paused every few feet to look upward for the orange-breasted robins, scarlet cardinals, and yellow finches she usually watched from her porch. Abbie listened for bird calls and chattered to the air and herself about wanting to be a pioneer like the women in the book. "It's like being an explorer," she declared, leaving the path and skipping toward an abandoned apple orchard. Miranda, her strange voice shrilly cutting across the quiet morning, ordered the child to stop, "I'm too old. Stay on the path. Come here. Come here."

"I see a bunny." Abbie was chasing the rabbit. Miranda watched the child disappear down a ravine. Miranda followed; her eyes focused mostly on her feet with the objective of staying on firm ground. "Please, my dear Lord, help me," she prayed.

Being an explorer became Abbie's ambition the second she thought of it. Filled with the romance of advancing her new fancy, the child dismissed the old woman's calls to stop. When they finally sat on a large rock near the crest of the hill, Miranda's small house was nowhere to be seen. Only the top of the flour mill was visible through the trees.

"I want to go home now." Miranda fixed Abbie's face in her hands so the child would pay attention, "Go home." Abbie shook her head "No." Her full-tilt imagination made her skin rosy, her small chest rise and fall with each deep breath. "More adventure," she said. And then with flamboyant stage gestures of a brave woman going on despite all odds, which the old woman could not decipher, Abbie was gone again. Miranda struggled off the rock and started after her excitable ward. "I'm hungry," Miranda pleaded, but the child was far too immersed in fantasy to listen.

Miranda angrily told the retreating child, "I'll tell your daddy and you'll get a spanking. You aren't minding." The rock-strewn earth might as well have been a mine field. She walked unsteadily and was relieved to find a small sturdy broken limb to use as a walking stick. With it she felt somewhat secure, although momentarily as she watched the strong-willed Abbie dash from one place to another Miranda wished she had found a switch instead. She stamped her foot on a smooth path of packed dirt and waved her stick-cane like a weapon. "Young lady, come here. You're in for it. I'm gonna tell your daddy. He'll beat your behind. He will."

The wind had picked up, rustling the leaves on the old apple trees, making the tall grass dance, and masking the sound of Miranda's high voice. Abbie stopped to pick yellow wild flowers her daddy called "sunshine dots," enabling the old woman to catch up. Just as Miranda angrily grabbed the child's arm, the mid-day sun was blocked by rolling clouds. The howling wind stopped suddenly and then it returned, just as suddenly, in alternating gusts of ice and heat. Miranda felt the thunder under her feet and was alarmed. But the electricity-charged air fueled Abbie. She took the old woman's hand and together they walked to a farmer's picnic spot. A three-sided shelter made of old barn boards stood next to a weeping willow. A small creek, swollen by rain upstream, meandered a few feet away.

They sat in the shelter at a picnic table, escaping the jumbo rain drops and pea-sized hail. Abbie got into the woman's lap. Facing her, she announced, "Now if we had some hot chocolate, we'd be in fine shape. Tomorrow, we'll get us some firewood. Make a fire."

"No." The answer was adamant.

The little girl wanting her way, gave her a hug. "Please play," she said into the wrinkled neck. The old woman observed the Kansas sky. She had experienced too many sudden Kansas storms to ignore the ominous green-gray, puffy clouds. The rains came down in sheets now and she knew that Little Turkey Creek would overflow soon, perhaps come up to the table where they sat and beyond. Although it was not cold, she shivered. She feared for the child in her care. She feared for the row of rooms that was her home in the storm-lashed valley. She feared for her reputation as a good and responsible Christian woman.

But Abbie was in her element. She was a brave pioneer, keeping her friend safe from the storm. When the roaring winds momentarily sucked away her breath and the sky turned to black, she could not see the sides of the small shelter. "It feels like I'm in a cave," she told herself. "I'm surrounded by wild animals which I will drive away."

Even when she began to realize Miranda was rigid with concern, the little girl was not alarmed. She refused to forfeit her fantasy until Miranda grabbed the child's hands and put them together, pushed her head forward and down. Huddled together they prayed the Lord's prayer until the leaves, branches and rain stopped swirling around them. The dirty cold creek water lapped at their feet and the sky grew lighter, making way for the sun.

The old woman and Abbie waded up to their ankles away from the rapidly rising water. At the crest of Turkey Creek Hill, no more than a city block or two away sat a farm house. "The Elmquists," said Miranda. The two arrived on the doorstep of the family just emerging from their cellar. Abbie whispered futilely to Miranda, "We pioneer women have been welcomed by Natives."

Mr. Elmquist hurried to them, catching the old woman as she stumbled. "My God," Mrs. Elmquist screamed. "My God, woman, what are doing out here? How did you get here?" the husband and wife practically carried an unsteady Miranda up the steps, while Janice, their daughter, took Abbie by the hand.

At the kitchen table, everyone watched Miranda, her eyes heavy, her shoulders slumped. "Child," barked Mrs. Elmquist, "tell us what happened. Now." Abbie told the story of their trek through the tall grass and the orchard, the final climb up Turkey Creek Hill. She talked about their shelter in the rain and praying. She left out the parts about the fleeing rabbit, the rising creek and, of course, any references to Miranda's objections. "It had to be at least six miles from her place to ours," Mr. Elmquist said. "Amazing."

Just then, the dozing Miranda sat up straight, grasping the table's edge with both hands. Perspiration spread across her forehead. Her mouth opened in a silent wail. Her eyes were staring in horror at an unseen truth.

"Get her help, the doctor," Mrs. Elmquist frantically instructed her husband.

Hours later when Miranda's pain had ceased and she was asleep, the doctor told them that the house the old woman had lived in for more than sixty years was done, destroyed by the storm.

"We'll tell her later, much later," Mr. Elmquist said. "You, Abbie, can stay here with us until your daddy comes home."

But Mrs. Elmquist, a natural accuser, shook her head at Abbie. "Why did you ever take the old woman on such a long walk? She's not well. Hasn't been since her heart attack before you were born. And the doctor thinks she may have had another one. Of all the stupid. . ."

Abbie tried to explain how she wanted an adventure and how the old woman led such a boring life. "She just reads and prays and sleeps. She doesn't even have a radio 'cause she can't hear one and I think she wanted to have fun, but she didn't know how. I don't think she has anyone to play with, and she can't really talk to people very well."

Janice pulled her chair closer to the child. "Well," she said, "it seems you saved the old woman's life. You got her out of her house before it blew away." Janice knew that was not so. Had the two eaten their lunch and returned to the front porch, which in the life of Miranda was inevitable, they would have seen the storm coming, could have taken refuge across the street in the basement of the Calvary Methodist Church and not only been safer, but a lot more comfortable.

"Where can she live now?" Abbie wanted to know. "Maybe she can live with Daddy and me."

"Maybe we'll just rebuild her house for her," said Mr. Elmquist.

"Or maybe she'll die first," grumbled his wife.

Janice arranged Abbie's bed on the living room couch and sat by her for a moment, stroking the little girl's head. "It's OK," she said. "Get some rest."

47

"We had an adventure," said the child. "Like pioneers." As sleep crept into the corners of her mind, Abbie envisioned herself saving lives as she rode west in a covered wagon. She dreamed about the picnic shelter which was now as long as a whole train. Her mother planted potatoes and cabbages at the top of the hill. She heard Miranda singing a song about spring in a clear, sweet voice as she washed their clothes in the creek. Her daddy sat at the table, covered with a red and white tablecloth, eating pies she had made of apples and cherries.

There was no rain.

A Traveling Man

Doris, it's Charlene, are you busy Hon? I can call back, but I want to run somethin' by ya.

Harve, I'm on the phone with Doris.

Oh, dang it. My ball and chain won't let me have a minute. Hang on, OK?

Anyway, OK, do you think that Alzheimers is, ya know, catching or does it get passed down from father to son and so on?

Yes, that's it—inherited. The reason I ask is ya know how Harve's dad was nutty as a fruitcake about the last ten years of his life. Remember him? He used to pinch you on the butt whenever you went with me over to take his lunch or somethin'.

That's not the worse of it, though. I sometimes think old men just get horny. Now, I haven't noticed Harve being that way unless you count the way he's always standing extra close to Ellen May Hulpepper during choir practice. Ever notice that? He says it's so he can read off her music like First Methodist doesn't have plenty of hymn books. Oh, Doris, hold on again. I swear. With Harve it's always somethin'.

Look under the sink, Harve. I always keep the rags under the sink. What are ya going to do? Harve, what are you going to clean?

I ask a question and he goes out the door. Oh, sometimes he burns me up. I suppose I shouldn't worry but last time he took a notion to do cleaning he ended up wiping down the inside of the garage with one of my best towels. Ya know the one I mean. I think you gave it to me for my birthday. A dark green with pink stripes? Big old fluffy thing. Oh, that's right, Aunt Erma gave it to me for an anniversary gift. Doesn't go in my bathroom and the green fuzz got all over me when I used it but that don't mean that it should be used to wipe dirt off a garage wall, does it?

My God, I just remembered another cleaning thing Harve did. Remember when he cleaned the dining room rug with Clorox. The kid was little and poured grape Kool-Aid on the gray rug that we bought at J.C. Penny when we lived in that rental on Grove Street. Remember that place? Little two-bedroom thing with a totally avocado green kitchen—stove, fridge, floor, everything painted what Harve called baby shit green. Well, as I told him, the rug would have been better with the purple on it instead of no color at all. Ended up putting it in our bedroom and putting the bed over the Clorox spot. Anyway, what do you think about Alzheimers and hereditary watchacallit?

See, Harve's old man kept forgetting stuff and then he started doing stuff. Ya know, he would put his toothbrush in the fridge or wander off somewhere. Once he went to Wichita on the bus. Just caught the bus and took off. Some waitress at the bus stop called Harve and told him to come get his old man. Lord knows what he thought he was doing, running away like that at his age. At least had the sense to show the waitress the card I filled out for his wallet. You know, name, phone number, next of kin?

He couldn't remember his wallet after a while though. Used to call you Rita, remember? Who the hell is Rita?

I swear. It's Harve again.

What do you want with the Black and Decker, Harve? Whatcha gonna clean up with that little vacuum cleaner? Can't it wait? In the hall closet up on the top shelf. Don't break it. Don't use it to clean up sand or somethin'.

So, Harve is really losing it. Gettin' on my nerves somethin' awful. He seems to remember names and where his toothbrush goes and all that, but he just gets in a fog. Stares at the TV or stands around in the back yard, talking to the dog. Somethin's goin on, Doris. Now, if it isn't Alzheimers, then it's somethin' else.

Last week he took his only good suit to the cleaners. I told him, Harve, if you're gonna do something like clean a perfectly clean suit, then at least have the decency to take along my lavender pants suit. Know that one, Doris, the one with the big silver buttons on the jacket? Hell, I've had it forever. Weren't you with me when I bought it at Sears on sale before the kid got married to that bimbo. Honestly, she's a sight. Her house is a mess and my grandson isn't any too bright. But what can you expect when the kid's mother smokes her brains out and watches soap operas all day? I ask ya. Does she get off her fanny to fix my son his breakfast? No. She's too busy working she says. Working at what? Picking up the remote?

Harve, I'm talking to Doris. The suitcase? What on earth do you want a suitcase for? It's down in the basement, next to the washer. Oh, for pity's sake.

A suitcase. Doris, I swear. First a cleaning frenzy and now a suitcase. Anyway, he's acting strange, kinda like he's a foreigner in a foreign country. Know what I mean? Doesn't seem to understand a thing I say.

Last night he said he was gonna read in bed. Well, I hooted at that. Haven't seen that man pick up a book since we went to high school and he had to make book reports for, what was her name? Old Wart Face is what we called her? Remember her? Oh, my God, Doris we've got Alzheimers. You and me both. Can't remember a teacher's name.

Anyway, he had gone to the library. Honest to Pete. And he checked out something about traveling on a budget. I asked him where he thought he was going and he just kept reading. Well, I said, at least consider taking me on this trip since you didn't consider taking my lavender pants suit to the cleaners. Hon, it went right over him. His daffy old dad lived to 85 which means if Harve is losing it, I got another 15 years of this aggravation. Know what I mean?

Now what? Doris, I just looked out the window and Harve is out there all dressed up to beat the band in his clean suit. And he's getting in the car which looks cleaner than it's looked in a coon's age. See what I mean? Nutty as his old dad.

Oh, well, bet ya a hundred dollars he's back in time for supper. Fixin' tuna casserole, my favorite. You always said it was my best dish. Harve doesn't much like it, but if I put potato chips on top, he'll eat it. Can't fix hamburger steak or pancakes everyday which he'd like just fine. Or catfish. God, I hate to fix catfish. Hate those little bones. If he's gonna forget stuff, I wish to heaven he'd forget about likin' catfish.

Well, this is choir practice night, so better get with it. Thanks for letting me bend your ear. Talk to ya later, Hon.

Oh, Doris, ya wanna go to Sears tomorrow? They're having a sale and I need me a new bathrobe. Maybe Harve can wear an old baggy flannel thing all the time, but I need a comfy robe to make me feel like a w-o-m-a-n.

Glad ya liked that. Hell, Harve wouldn't catch on.

JOURNEY WITH NO SOUND

It was as if you were listening
 to lightening infected radio
with timed volume. On the train
you watched running horses,
placed your hands on the windows
to absorb sounds.

You crawled and walked but did not speak
until we put plastic in your ears,
turned on the box you wore,
taught you to read our mouths,
words, and kisses.

When you were five, you summoned a poem
about the sun on your face, the river water
cooling your feet and how your head
was just the right size for your body.
You saw us watching and smiled,
adept at joy and grace before we were.

VISTAS

PICTURE WINDOW

Life does not hang in a museum.
It does not decorate a wall or wait on an easel.
Life is framed by windows, doors.

A wooden frame borders
my brick street, the back of a late-model
car, partial tree trunk affixed to earth.
When the window is blinded,
night drops on my front yard.

Then I will eat my supper egg,
look upon another scene.
A wider view of passing car beams,
children calling a wayward dog.

Toward midnight I will sleep
in my lover's arms.
In the vapor of dreams, I will see him
from my window on a gilt-edged afternoon,
as he climbed the stairs to my front door.

GARDEN'S HEX

Showers promise April tulips.
The sun blesses yellow ones.
Red and pink stand tallest.
White sway in the breeze.
Wine tulips lift their throats to drink.

The butterfly bushes grow beyond belief.
They birth lavender blooms.
Thin sturdy limbs balance leaves
and give landing space
to pastel dancing wings.

But the pansies do not comply.
The hope for a mixed bed
of three petals framing tiny faces
dies before the new moon
above the garden's terrain.

CITYSCAPE

You and I
on our fire escape
the city closing us off
from soil and sky
except for one star
brighter than the rest
that sparkled like
a jazz riff.

UNTITLED

The lake sleeps under Thomas Hart Benton sky.
Worried buck and doe bolt for cover.
Behind the cabin's window you look inward,
back hunched in anger.
I will stay away staring at fading light
until fore-warned rain comes in water pebbles,
forces me to decide between breeching your solitude
or racing like a disquieted deer to closed room.
I choose you.
We watch puffy clouds deflate, lose their gray,
rippling breezes rouse the lake.
Moonlight smiles at familiar deer sipping coolness.
Tomorrow they will come back, as will we.

1953 Wellington Wheat Festival

August's void of evening breezes
capped a small park gorged with crowds.
Ride lights were glimmering circles,
teasing children with no tickets.
I envied friends certain of their beauty,
practiced in promoting romance.
A dreamer unsure of her dreams,
shy as a colt, afraid of my yearnings,
I pretended apathy toward the boy,
eyes smiling, who stood before me.
Today memory comes in cloud wisps,
but long ago under a luminous sky,
I clearly recall the handsome boy
who held my hand and walked me home.
I still smell the oil in his hair,
and hear the band play "Tenderly."

THE WINDOW CLOSED TO SNOW

revealed a fox curled on cast gray ground,
full tail draped round,
pointed nose resting on paws
and brazen jet eyes judging
me. He disdained,
I think, my gaze mistook for avarice.

He told me he was his own fox. To wrap
myself in a blanket, leave him
to stretch and search
for a rodent fat on grain
spilled in the barn, or a rabbit,
white hiding under snow knoll
built on scrub oak. An egg
left alone for pecking time.

A cup of tea and down comforter
took me from the view to ponder
fate, the fox and smaller, soft-eyed beings
searching too.

THE SEWING ROOM

When Danny's high school graduation picture reappeared on the mantle, Joe chose silence, just as he had when Mildred removed it from the same place almost two years earlier. They had traversed sorrow on different paths.

"I want a sewing room," Mildred told her husband the day after the picture vanished. Joe carried his wife's sewing machine from the glassed-in porch into Danny's room. Several relatives told themselves how little time had passed before Mildred called in a workman to paint over the blue walls, pull up the old gray carpet and replace the shutters with curtains.

Neighbors noticed the premature arrival of a Salvation Army truck backed into the driveway, swallowing up a boy's bed, chairs, and desk. Danny's aunt chastised her sister for so quickly dismantling his room, as did Joe's mother. Joe hushed them both. "Let her grieve her own way," he told them.

"It will be a good place to read and do my work, darning, and quilting, you know," she said. "It will be an uneventful place. Restful, I think. Peaceful." He smiled and patted her arm.

"A place like your den is for you." She sounded harsher than she had intended. He unnerved her with his constant kindness.

That night in bed, she further divulged her intent. "Just as I don't come into your den, because it is yours," she told him gently, "please let me have my room, my sewing room for myself." Joe held her hand and said he would stay outside, just as she wished. Mildred took her hand away to pull the covers closer.

He had long appreciated his own place where she never cleaned up after him or rearranged his papers. Where she didn't fret over water rings on his desk or dirty coffee cups by his recliner. Yet she was welcome to visit him there, to sit in his recliner and chat about the day. She had many times. But not since the accident. Self-exiled, she made no attempt to take the portrait of a gawky, endearing fourteen-year-old Danny from the wall behind Joe's desk.

He respected her request except for one time, when he was searching for a needle and thread while she was away visiting an elderly aunt. Just as he had never admitted to his wife that he missed seeing the mantle picture of a young man in cap and gown, he never told her of his one transgression, his single invasion into her own place. He never told her how much he saw in the few seconds he stood clutching a button from his good blue shirt.

On the old card table covered with her grandmother's lace shawl was the missing graduation picture and a dozen others, arranged around Danny's senior yearbook. Pictures of Danny as a baby, as a buck-toothed six-year-old and Danny with braces. Danny at Christmas when he was four, tearfully making certain his father knew that the training wheels on his new red bike would have to go. The Halloween when he went trick or treating as Superman. Danny fishing with his father, clowning with his prom date, sitting with his mother in a canoe when the family vacationed in Alaska. Proud Danny in his football jersey.

Hanging on a hall tree next to the table were his letter jacket and the K-State sweatshirt his Uncle Don gave him to wear at college. In a dark metal frame on the wall was the front-page story of the accident with its horrifying picture of the car twisted and broken and the headline about a graduation party.

The shrine extended to a board-and-brick bookshelf and his Lincoln logs, a Fisher-Price farm, and a big yellow truck he had played with for hours in the backyard sand pile. A baseball glove and textbooks, favorite albums, a root-beer mug, and his size 13 tennis shoes. The remains of his life were neatly arranged in his mother's sewing room.

When, many months later, Danny's graduation picture came back to its mantle place, Joe didn't have to look to know that the shrine had been taken down, that their son's mementos had been put in the newly taped boxes he had carried for her to the basement storage room.

That night, Mildred told him, "I'd like a small sofa in Danny's old room and the television, too. We could drink coffee and watch the news together. Or play records of songs we used to dance to in college."

"I think that would be very nice," Joe said.

"Do you mind if I decorate a bit, new carpet and wallpaper, that sort of thing?"

Joe took her hand. "I'd like that."

Mildred pulled his hand to her lips. "It will be a nice room. Restful and peaceful."

A BUD

velvet
stem bound
lives
intrepidly
blossoming
grows
with seasons
sleeps, blooms
unless
cast in a vase
shrouded by shadows
senselessly
in fetid water
petals brown
dies
of heedless act
denying death's timing.

SPIDER TRACKS

Sun nor moon can reach beneath
the porch amid garden tool clutter
where spiders hide, skate
over leaves blown into hoary piles.
Their dinners amble into woven lairs.
If some unseen hand could wash
away the spider of my soul,
if that could be, I'd wait in darkness
at the precipice, watch them
struggle against the current.

VISTA

Foothills of soiled white
crisscross pillow cliffs.
Blankets blizzard the cold bed,
messy with old ifs.

Morning sun-streaks
from a triangle on the carpet,
points to the V of me, legs
akimbo, where I sit.

My thoughts are soaked
in last night's wine
and lost to murky dreams
of missing time.

No promise held beyond
a glass of chardonnay
and chilly hills of sheets
on another winter day.

FAMILY TRUST

Should be robin orange breast.
Skewed vision is no excuse.
Here's another thing.
Dad was blue and passed it on.
We children found niches in gray,
away from his mean wit.
Away from our mother in white
who believed in duty, also a lie.
From their graves, Mother and Father call
at inconvenient times, insist
on staying for meals.
He wraps his wrath in cold night air
while she pretends first light. The truth
is where a tributary once fed a fountain.
Where mingling hues meld
in memories, fade, and swirl.
Where robins come to rest in budding elms.

TO FALL

I fall away from skies
too blue to bear, light
on bed of leaves or on stacks
of hay, summer mown
in barn striped with sunlight.
Fall kick starts life.
Apples float. Colors
flare in maple, mums.
Monarchs fly above fields
plow-ridged awaiting seeds, rain.
When early dark wraps itself
outside a familiar quilt,
cedar scented, patched
for winter's resolve.
I fall away.

GRANDAD'S GATELESS FENCE

I built a fence yesterday, three plywood pieces
affixed to each other, then to the back of the garage.
I like what I've made from recycled wood
and rusty nails left in a coffee can under the porch.
Might paint the boards to match the house.

From back door to fence, I made a path of river rock,
some from a nursery, some from fishing trips
before my wife died beside me in our bed.
If she could see what I've done, she'd tsk, tsk me.
Ask why I'd put something without a way in or out.

I'd argue for a compost pile, though I don't garden,
I know it's not a place for a dog or chickens.
Nor for bushes that grow unruly without pruning.
I tell you, it's easy to build a gateless fence,
wearisome to figure what to do with it later.

UDALL, KANSAS

May 25, 1955

The man uneasy left their bed.
His wife sleeping on her back
hands crossed at her neck clutching
a linen sheet as if it might escape.
Air hot and cold weighed heavy
on his chest, stole his breath.
At 10:30 he checked TV and radio,
got static for his efforts.
A calico paced up and down stairs,
Mewling as if calling lost kittens.
The man and cat were students of storms,
big and not, sent each spring to Kansas.
He couldn't see out the kitchen door
unless lightening zigged and zagged,
through bolts that made shadows
of the grain elevator and water tower.
A train whistle blew and blew.
The man feared the engineer
meant a warning because he saw evil drop,
turn earth into debris as it charged toward town.

The news at ten issued all clear
so he had assumed only a thunderstorm.
Now he thought he'd better call his wife,
secure them both beneath the kitchen table.
By then it was 10:35
and the most powerful Kansas tornado ever,
bore down on Udall with whistling, roaring
homicidal winds bent on fostering hell.
Dawn covered the awful results with pale light.
Silence wandered like a ghost
amid uprooted trees planted a hundred years ago,
houses without roofs and doors,
a telephone pole piercing the side of a church,
broken glass filling a bathtub.
Rescuers found death and affliction
in rooms without walls, flattened cars,
fields stripped of crops, flooded spaces.
The calico cat hid under a rain-soaked sofa.
No one found the man or his wife,
their house cleaved into splinters.
Reporters and cameramen hastened into the town
to find their story. Amid the ruins
one of them wrote, "The little town of Udall
died in its sleep last night."

REFLECTIONS

BACKSLIDING LIBERAL

The incessant down low, loud
whump, whump, whump from
the boy's cherry red pickup
makes me rethink my opposition
to capital punishment.

A Time for Dancing

Soon you'll get Medicare. More
money for prescriptions, less
for the insurance company. Fewer
trips to Europe until we win the lottery.
Our joke. We eschew fairy tales
although we agree our marriage survives
despite wicked witches, travails
through forests of snaking trees, darkness,
briars that scratched thin skin.
Autumn closes in now. Cool air whisks
past the patio door we will shut soon.
You will light a fire. I will burn a candle
smelling of lavender and one of lemon.
We will play Sinatra and Rosemary,
The Four Freshmen and Tormé.
Days will shorten as we two-step. It is time.
And we are grateful for it.

Writing while Walking

Focus on commonplace.
Do so uncommonly.
Leaves dancing on stoic branches.
Cracks creating abstract art
on a sidewalk canvas.
Inhale the aroma of someone's supper
mingling with lilacs and the orange you ate
still perfuming lips and fingers.
Take in the sun lounging on its side
telegraphing sunset colors of rose and peach.
Notice tree shadows as sentinels,
bushes replicating crouching people,
all the curtained windows in a house,
a patchwork quilt. Hear bird songs
receding into evening's quieter refrain
of symphonic insects tuning
their instruments. Watch a twinkling airplane
sliding across a berry blue sky.

THE SAFEST BET

is to stay burrowed
close to our roots.
But what if we choose
to gun the motor, zigzag
upward, downward
until rescinding horizons dull.

In the dark we will confront cliffs
to fall off, plains to nod off,
deserts without water,
swamps with too much.
Ghettos with drugs
and suburbs with disdain.

How do we know
the farmer isn't the flim flam man,
the teacher a pederast,
the preacher a teller of tales,
the mother a whore?
How do we know our station
since we come from the womb
without vita or flag?

Answers slither. Time speeds.
If you won't go, I'll go it alone
as was intended somewhere by someone
not interested in details,
wouldn't share them anyway.

THE CORE OF SILENCE

Silence cannot compete with howl
and growl of thoughtless dogs.
I pause in my walk to create metaphors
on the back of milk, sweet peas, soup crackers list.
Behind a fence, a barking dog
dispatches my spirit aloft
and back with a thud.
Through dinner the din from widow's dearest
in rhinestone collar, slices through Gershwin.
Dozing, book resting on my belly,
a baying beagle assaults respite,
calls for regard from the moon.

Now That I Am Older

I am no longer

a camera

a driver

a ringing phone

I no longer

remember details to my tales

recall the books I've read

routinely speak in present tense

recover all I've misplaced

I am

Dorothy asleep in black and white

Wile E. Coyote suspended in space

DROWNING IN DEPRESSION

Nothing dark (despite assertions by poets),
but a colorless mass that weighs
upon my chest, pinches, and twists. A scrim
slumps on my eyelids. Anchored
body sinks below life.

Endure, I beg. This is not death.
Remember the truth.
Soon my eyes will
open, seek hues. I will become light
and swim in it. Welcome back
my thwarted spirit. Do what
I can before my colors fade again.

COVENANT

I watch and am as a sparrow alone on the house top.
                                        Psalm 102:7

Once hubris burled me skyward,
conceit caught the Milky Way.
I could dance on a star,
kiss the sunrise, too. Look
down and not get dizzy.
But gravity lunged,
pulled me back, set me
as a sparrow solo
on a roof top, made me hear grief,
drink tears.

Some say God created endurance,
freed the prisoner, sent the pelican
to the fish-filled sea. Promised
to stick around even when I fly
too high to see the Earth,
fall too low to embrace
the in between.

Recurring Dreams

Dreams hold my feet (I cannot run)
silence sound (I cannot scream).
I am not the only one late to class
who cannot recall a locker combination,
and if I could, do not know where to go
or what time to be there.
I am not the only one who falls from great heights,
is lost in a forest, a city's winding streets.
Nor am I the only nude at a formal party.
I try to shrug off discomfort born in sleep
leave interpretation to Freudians and parlor gamers.
It doesn't matter if I am not alone
when dreams foment fear (I cannot define)
kidnap peace (I cannot find).

MODERNITY

Like a woman wearing too much rouge,
it is unnatural to stand in line with food
wrapped in cellophane and encased in cans.
Shouldn't we be on our knees,
waving aside flying bugs and pulling
beets from the soil? Wouldn't it be best
to rest our eyes on blooms and birds
rather than a story about alien space
babies and super stars who dangle
them from balconies? Keeping up has led us down
the shopping aisle to computer check outs,
has blocked the path to feed the chickens,
hell bent as we are on decorum. I ask you,
why do we trade dust between our toes
for summer sandals that require a pedicure?
Trade a rabbit munching lettuce for chatty clerks
who forget to wrap meat
so blood seeps into paper or plastic,
as we choose?

BIRTHSTONE

According to mythology, Diana turned a young woman,
Amethyst, to quartz, saving her from the God of wine.

Your earrings are the real deal,
my sister told me on Christmas Day.
Don't lose one. She knows
I can be careless. Two stones,
twilight hued, with tiny diamonds
on top, stars navigating. Her
gesture gives me serenity.
I know for whom the stones
are named. True, she did not think
my February jewels were more
than her love although she knew
my penchant for wine and how long
I'd avoided its lure. I vow
these gems will not be lost.
They signal the end to winter's storms,
welcome the lilac's bloom.

AUTHOR NOTE

The poems and short stories contained in this book comprise a collection of work produced over decades. While attempts to track down all the original publishers of individual poems and stories were successful, please accept apologies for any errors or omissions. The author gratefully acknowledges the editors and publishers who first printed the following:

"Before It Gets Dark" in *Everyday Tales,* Lindsborg Arts Council 1999

"To Fall" and "The Window Closed to Snow," *Poetry of Kansas 2003*

The poems included in the chapbook *Ironing Out the Wrinkles 2003*

"The Sewing Room," *Byline Magazine* November 2005

"Journey With No Sound" a winning entry in *Kansas Voices* contest, Winfield Arts and Humanities Council 2005-2009

"1953 Wellington Wheat Festival," *The Coop: A Poetry Cooperative,* https://150kansaspoems.wordpress.com/ April 2015

"Udall, Kansas" in *Kansas Time+Space: An Anthology of Heartland Poetry,* Little Balkans Press 2017

ACKNOWLEDGEMENTS

When I wrote my first chapbook, Sarah Bagby, owner of Watermark Books and Café, gave me space and time to do readings and sell my books. She was always there to offer to sell my writing and give me an audience. She brings vitality to the literary life of Wichita. Thank you Sarah.

The late Colleen Kelly Johnston, who was actively involved in Wichita civic and family activities, was also an accomplished writer. A friend, Colleen invited me to join her poetry group. She was the first person who told me I could write poetry — and then encouraged me to do so.

Thank you to the many women and men who shared their expertise in poetry and prose in the writing groups I joined. You were gracious with your patience and your comments. Your support provided a safe place to read and discuss our latest writings and provided constructive feedback to shape our work. Special thanks goes to Roy J. Beckemeyer, one of those writing group colleagues, for his perfect Foreword to this book.

This book would not have happened without the skill and patience of Charlotte Crawford at Post Rock Press.

About the Author

Myrne Roe has had a series of careers that would be enough for five people. She is a former teacher, congressional chief of staff, Wichita State University public relations and marketing executive, editorial writer, and nationally syndicated columnist. Winner of numerous awards for her poetry, she has compiled and edited several anthologies about Kansas people. *Radiating Like a Stone: Wichita Women and the 1970s Feminist Movement* is a gold mine of the history of Wichita women. Now, as an octogenarian, she has gathered some of her poems and short stories, reflecting her career. She was married to the late Jon Roe for 59 years; they have a son, Matthew.

22459335R00063